Where's Bear?

Hilary McKay

illustrated by Alex Ayliffe

Margaret K. McElderry Books

To Jim and Snowy
—H. M.

For James and Millie
—A. A.

Margaret K. McElderry Books
An imprint of Simon & Schuster Children's Publishing Division
1230 Avenue of the Americas
New York, New York 10020

Text copyright © 1998 by Hilary McKay
Illustrations copyright © 1998 by Alex Ayliffe

First US Edition 1998
Printed in Belgium
10 9 8 7 6 5 4 3 2 1

Library of Congress Catalog Card Number: 98-65819
ISBN 0-689-82271-5

Once upon a time there was a bear and a boy.
The boy's name was Simon, and he was very young.
He could only say three words:
"Where gone, Snowtop?"
Snowtop was the bear.

Snowtop's fur was partly soft and partly hard and sticky.
Between his ears and under his chin he was snow white,
but the rest of him was pale gray with patches.
The patches were all sorts of colors . . .

wet grass color . . .

sandbox color . . .

leaky paint box and jam color . . .

a color that came from the
scary place under the stairs where
the rubber boots were kept.

Snowtop had a
wonderful Snowtop smell.
Simon thought he was the
most beautiful bear
in the world.

One day, Simon's grandmother came to visit.
She hugged Simon and she hugged
his mother and then she said,
"My goodness! Just look at Snowtop!"
So everyone looked at Snowtop.
Then Gran and Simon's mother went
into the kitchen and talked quietly
to each other.

All at once Gran came running back.
"Hurry up! Hurry up!" she called to Simon. "We're going out!
Wipe your face! Put on your shoes! Quick, quick, while the
sun is shining!"

Before Simon had time to think,
he was galloping along the road
beside Gran, their coats and bags
and mouths all flapping with
hurry and excitement.
Simon had never guessed that
his gran could run so fast.

They overtook walkers and
shoppers and bikers and joggers.
They passed a little girl
carrying a bear.
"Where gone, Snowto—?"
began Simon suddenly.
"Stop! Stop!" said Gran.
"Here is the toy store!"

The toy store was exciting.

"Try everything!" said Gran. "It's that sort of store!"
So Simon tried trains and drums and slides and trampolines, and
he looked at books and blocks and a whole shelf of beautiful be—
"Where *gone*, Snowt—?" asked Simon.
"Hurry! Hurry!" said Gran. "And we'll have time to go to the fair!
Quick, quick, while the sun is shining!"

The treat was delicious.

Soda and ice cream and sausages
and chips and marshmallow cakes
shaped like lovely white be—
"Where gone, Sno—?"
roared Simon all of a sudden.

"Quick! Quick!" said Gran.
"We must get home before dark!"
And she ran Simon home so fast
that he hardly had time to breathe.

Strange Bear was soft and fluffy
and white and smelled of soap.
Simon dropped Strange Bear and cried,
"Where gone, Snowtop?
Where gone, Snowtop?"

And he continued
to howl these sad
words all through
suppertime . . .

and bathtime . . .

and storytime.
Gran and his mother
did not run and fetch Snowtop.

They gave him Strange Bear instead.
Also, they laughed.

Strange Bear did not laugh.
When bedtime came, Simon found him sitting on his pillow.

Simon hurled Strange Bear onto the floor, howled,
"Where gone, Snowtop?" one more time, and fell asleep.

In the middle of the night, Simon woke up. Strange Bear was lying on the floor looking at him. "Where gone, Snowtop?" whispered Simon, and he climbed out of bed because suddenly he could not stand one more minute without going to look for him.

It was very dark outside the bedroom door. Simon looked at the dark, and then he looked back into his bedroom, and there was Strange Bear looking very brave and friendly, despite his soapy whiteness.

So Strange Bear and Simon went
to hunt for Snowtop together.

They looked everywhere.

They looked
in the toy box.

They crawled under tables.

They sneaked outside
across the wet grass.

They dug for Snowtop
in the sandbox.

They even looked in the scary
place under the stairs
where the rubber
boots were kept.

Then suddenly it was morning.

"Where gone . . . ?" murmured Simon sleepily, and opened
his eyes. And there in his arms was Snowtop.
There he was, Snowtop, with fur that was partly soft
and partly hard and sticky, and pale gray with patches.
And he had the same wonderful Snowtop smell
that Simon remembered so well.

But Strange Bear had vanished, and Simon was sorry.

Simon and Snowtop searched for Strange Bear.
Simon thought that if Gran ever took him to the toy store
and the fair and for ice cream and cake
all in one afternoon again,
then Strange Bear might come back.
But Gran never did.
She said it wasn't worth it.
She didn't seem pleased that
Snowtop was back.

But Simon was pleased, because Snowtop was the most
beautiful bear in the world.
He had brave, friendly eyes, just like Strange Bear,
but he wasn't white and fluffy . . .

. . . and he didn't smell of soap.